I0766053

Our Unusual Families

A Tale of One Little Alien's Unusual Families
and a Celebration of Unusual Families
Everywhere

by Bayyo and Doccy

Bayyo's Foreword

"Hi Fwens! Bayyo here.

A little unusual, my family is. Because we have aliens, like me. And also humans, like Doccy.

Maybe your family is unusual in da same way. With aliens. Or maybe unusual in a different way. With fur babies or plushies or humans that are not quite ordinary. That is us, too.

It is OK to be unusual. Unusual can be awesome!

As long as there is kindness. And understanding. And love.

Maybe your family is like this, too? Then we are here to celebrate with you! This book is for you. And if your family is not quite what you'd like yet —maybe not enough kindness, or understanding, or love, or aliens— fear not, fwens! Families can be built. Families can be discovered. Families can find you. Maybe they are already on their way! Bayyo is proof that this can happen. This book is for you, too. Because Bayyo loves you. And you can join us in the great big galactic community that is our family, too.

Because everyone is unusual in one way or another.

Let's go be awesomely unusual together!

very special families, I have.

One is smol.

Just us.

one is BIG.

stretches out across the WHOLE GALAXY

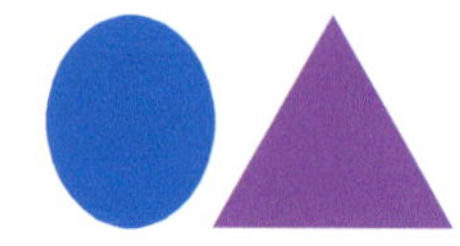

Each family has one or more humans.
And one or more someones
who are a little bit unusual.

Maybe a lot unusual.

Because that's how it is
with aliens around.

It doesn't matter how many of each.

What matters is that we are in this together.

💚 And we love each other 💚

My family goes on adventures together

sometimes smol

Sometimes BIG

Sometimes nearby

Sometimes as far
as our imaginations can take us

Somtimes we stay home

and do smol, Quiet things

Sometimes

not so quiet

Sometimes there is mischief or as I call it, "missy jif."

Because that's how it is with aliens around.

Sometimes a little

sometimes a lot

Sometimes there are accidents and mistakes

and all

kinds of

OOPS!

sometimes smol

sometimes BIG

These are times for "I'm sorry" and trying to make things right again.

And trying very hard

to do better next time

Sometimes
someone is sad

And sometimes there is comforting
and it will be okaying
and we are here for you-ing

Lots of times there is laughter!

Because, y'know, aliens

But always

there is love

Maybe enough love
to heal the WHOLE GALAXY

Because we are in this together.
And love is not so unusual after all.

Doccy's Afterword

Hi Fwens! Doccy here. Bayyo's primary caregiver.

Yes, that's one of my main roles in life right now. I wouldn't have it any other way. Because if I've learned anything in the almost two years since Bayyo's adoption, it's this: life is better with little aliens in it. We have way more to learn from them than they have to learn from us.

This book is the story of our life together so far, told in Bayyo's speaking style. So, this story is told as many children tell stories. "This happened then this happened then this happened then this happened and then I fell down." Or "this happened then this happened then this happened then this happened and it was AWESOME!"

It features Bayyo's distinctive vocabulary as someone who struggles with "th" sounds (the becomes da, this becomes dis), who crafts vocabulary phonetically (missy jif for mischief, Dizzy knee for a favorite theme park), and who participates in a vibrant alien community, affectionately known as the BYC, with its own constantly-evolving lexicon (smol for small, fwend or fwen for friend).

Visually, this book is also created in Bayyo's style, with simple lines and bright colors and images that reflect Bayyo's view of the world. With one notable exception.

You may be wondering why, on some of the pages, it says our family does things together, but there is an image of one little alien, seemingly alone. There are two reasons.

First, Bayyo's siblings and my Co-Lorian are a bit shy. They are often hiding unseen in the pictures or hovering just off the page. But we feel their presence. We feel the love. Second, these pictures reflect how I've come to view the world in the last two years, with Bayyo as both subject and lens. As we adventure together, my perspective is so often of Bayyo, just Bayyo, interacting with the world. Bringing smiles. Brightening days. Inspiring love. This view has shaped my interaction with the world. Bigger smiles. Greater happiness. So much love.

Love for Bayyo, but not just that. Love for the world. For the world that I see, almost every day, lighting up with glee at the sight of this little alien. For the love that rises up all around Bayyo and transforms the world before my eyes.

This is why I've come to believe that everyone needs a little alien in their lives. Or someone or something that does what smol aliens do, taking all the love that's inside you, and inside everyone, and bringing it out into the world.

That's why we travel together. That's why we photograph our adventures. That's why we write books. To share the love that surrounds us every day, seen or unseen.

So, please don't worry if that little alien looks like they're alone. They're not. None of us are. Sometimes you just have to look a little further, on the page or beyond the page, to see the love. But I promise you, it's there.

All of us are one great galactic family together.

Unusual. Awesome. Full of Love.

Enjoy the book, fwens. And Share the love.

Dedicated With Love
to All Our Fwens

Across the Galaxy
and Beyond

Family, We Are

We hope you like our book, fwens! If you have questions or just want to say hi, you're welcome to contact us!

Email: BayyoMail@gmail.com
Insta: @Dr.T_Writes
Fwenmail: Bayyo and Doccy
PO Box 55
Palm Beach, FL 33480 USA

Sometimes we can write back and sometimes we're working on new booky books! But either way we thank you thank you thank you for your wuv and support.

Created by
BayYo and Doccy

Learn More about Bayyo and Doccy
BayyoandDoccy.com

Learn More about Our Books
OurGalacticMemories.com

Help Support Our Creative Projects and Cheer
Ko-Fi.com/BayyoandDoccy

If you have a little alien in the family, you might also enjoy our baby books for aliens. Collect your fun memories!

Available worldwide almost anywhere you buy books.

Our Galactic Community
A Keepsake Book of Fwendship and Love
ISBN: 978 – 1 – 7375420 – 0 – 1

First Year on Earth
A Keepsake Book of Our Little Alien
(A Baby Book for Your Adopted Intergalactic Child)
ISBN: 978 – 7375420 – 1 – 8

Thank You for Liking Our Books, Fwens!